GOOD NIGHT OWL

For Susan Viguers

ISBN 978-1-338-11654-0

12 11 10 9 8 7 6 5 4 3 2 1   16 17 18 19 20 21

Printed in the U.S.A.   08

First Scholastic printing, September 2016

GOOD NIGHT OWL

GREG PIZZOLI

SCHOLASTIC INC.

Owl was settling into bed
when he heard a noise.

It was a tiny sound,
no louder than a whisper;
a funny noise
he hadn't heard before.

"Someone must be at the door," said Owl.
"Just a minute!"

But no one was there.

"Probably the wind," said Owl.

And he lay down in bed, and said
to himself, "Good night, Owl."

SQUEEK!

Then he heard the noise again.

"It's coming from the cupboard," said Owl.

So he went to take a look.

He emptied every shelf,

but there was no noise to be found.

So Owl went back to bed.

"Good night, Owl," he said.

And then he heard the noise.

SQUEEK!

"It must be under the floor," said Owl.

And he pulled up the floorboards,

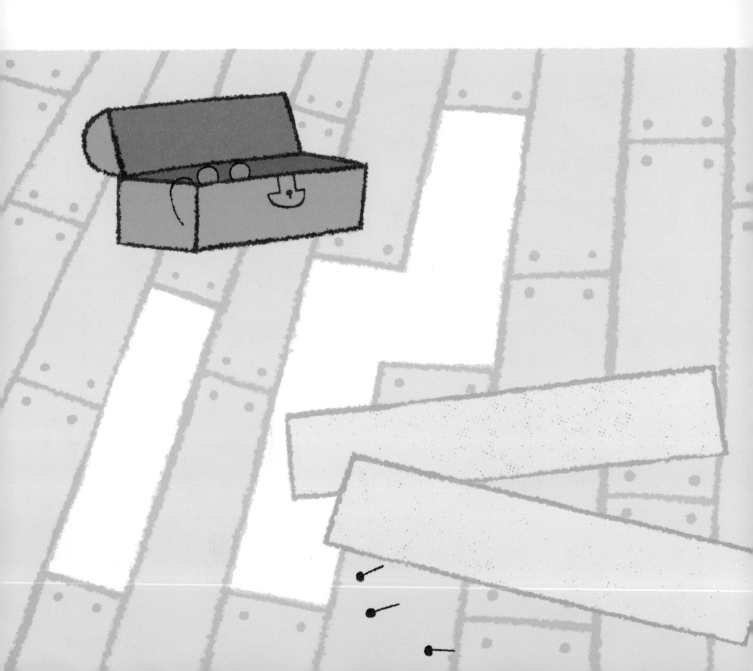

one by one.

But he didn't find the noise.

So Owl went back to bed.

SQUEEK!

"This house has a noisy roof!" yelled Owl.

And he took down the roof.

"There!" said Owl.
"No more noise!"

Owl got back into bed,
the stars and the moon
shining down where his roof
used to be.

"Good night, Owl," he said.

But Owl didn't close his eyes—
he didn't dare.

He knew that any second
he would hear the noise.

He waited . . .

and waited . . .

and waited . . .

and waited.

SQUEEK?

"It's in the walls!" Owl screeched.

"I'll get you, noise!" Owl said

as he tore down the walls of his house.

But he found nothing.
The cupboard was empty,
the floorboards were pulled up,
the roof was pulled down,
and the walls were gone.

Owl went back to bed,
and he said, "Good night, Owl."

And then he saw the noise.

SQUEEK

Owl smiled.
He said, "Good night, noise."

And they went to sleep.